HOLLY KELLER

Furry

GREENWILLOW BOOKS, NEW YORK

Watercolor paints and a black pen
were used for the full-color art.
The text type is ITC Barcelona Medium.

Printed in Singapore by Tien Wah Press
First Edition   10 9 8 7 6 5 4 3 2 1

Library of Congress Cataloging-in-Publication Data
Keller, Holly.
  Furry / by Holly Keller.
    p.   cm.
  Summary: Laura's allergies make it difficult
for her to find a pet she likes, until her
brother brings home a surprise.
  ISBN 0-688-10519-X (trade).
ISBN 0-688-10520-3 (lib.)
(1. Pets—Fiction.   2. Allergy—Fiction.
3. Anoles—Fiction.)   I. Title.
PZ7.K28132Fu   1992
(E)—dc20   90-24645   CIP   AC

FOR ANNETTE
AND JEFF,

SOME YEARS LATER

Laura wanted a pet.
First Mama said, "No," and Papa said, "No."
Then Mama said, "Maybe," and Papa said nothing.
So Laura waited.

But when Mrs. Bentley's dog had
puppies, and Laura hugged
and petted them, she sneezed
until her nose was red and sore.

When Alfie found a kitten in the schoolyard
and brought him home "for keeps,"
Laura's eyes began to tear,
and Alfie gave the kitten to their neighbor.

The new bunnies in the science room
made Laura break out in a rash.

And Gloria Goldberg's guinea pigs
made her wheeze.

When Bennie brought his gerbil into
school for show-and-tell,
Laura's face swelled up like a balloon.

Even Ellen's parakeets made
her head ache.

"It's allergies," Dr. Cooper said.
"Don't get too close to birds
or pets with fur."
And Laura cried.

The next day Alfie caught a bullfrog in the pond.
"You can have him for a pet," he told Laura.
But Laura wouldn't look at it.

Alfie's friend Susan said Laura
could have her water snake,
but Laura screamed and ran
inside the house.

"A goldfish would be nice," Mama said.
"Or a turtle," Papa suggested.
  But Laura shook her head.
"Only pets with fur are fun," she said.
  And Laura moped.

Then Alfie saw a picture in a magazine
that gave him an idea.
He whispered it to Mama, who said, "No."
Then he told it to Papa, who said, "Maybe."

And on Saturday Alfie and Papa
went to the pet store.

"What is it?" Laura asked when Alfie
put the box on the table.
"A pet," Alfie said, and Laura frowned.
She opened the box a crack and
looked inside.

"Ugh," she said loudly,
and she slammed the lid shut.
"It looks like a dragon with measles."

"You have to watch him," Alfie said.
So Laura watched.

"Okay, Alfie," Laura said.
"How did you do that?"
Alfie smiled.

Laura ran her fingers down
the little chameleon's back.
"Wow," she said out loud,
and Mama laughed.

"He needs a good name," Papa said.
"FURRY," Alfie blurted out,
    and this time even Laura laughed.

"Do you like him?" Alfie asked.
"Yes," Mama said.
"Yes," Papa said.
And Laura said, "Maybe."

"Can he sleep in my room?"
Laura asked.
"Of course," Mama said.
And after dinner Laura took
Furry upstairs.